ZOMBIEFIED!

C.M. GRAY

ABC
Books

The ABC 'Wave' device is a trademark of the Australian Broadcasting Corporation and is used under licence by HarperCollins*Publishers* Australia.

First published in Australia in 2015
by HarperCollins *Children's Books*
a division of HarperCollins*Publishers* Australia Pty Limited
ABN 36 009 913 517
harpercollins.com.au

HarperCollins*Publishers*
Level 13, 201 Elizabeth Street, Sydney NSW 2000, Australia
Unit D1, 63 Apollo Drive, Rosedale, Auckland 0632, New Zealand
A 53, Sector 57, Noida, UP, India
1 London Bridge Street, London, SE1 9GF, United Kingdom
2 Bloor Street East, 20th floor, Toronto, Ontario M4W 1A8, Canada
195 Broadway, New York NY 10007, USA

National Library of Australia Cataloguing-in-Publication entry:

Gray, C.M. author.
  Zombiefied! / C.M. Gray.
  978 0 7333 3421 4 (pbk.)
  978 1 4607 0492 9 (ebook)
  For primary school age.
  Zombies — Juvenile fiction.
  Suspense fiction.
A823.4

Cover design by Hazel Lam, HarperCollins Design Studio
Cover and internal illustrations by C.M. Gray
Printed and bound in Australia by Griffin Press
The papers used by HarperCollins in the manufacture of this book are
a natural, recyclable product made from wood grown in sustainable
plantation forests. The fibre source and manufacturing processes meet
recognised international environmental standards, and carry certification.

For Jasper and Lucas
★MWAH! MWAH!★
(Yes, you both just got a kiss
from Mum in public.)

1

'Watch out! Behind you!'

The zombie came out of nowhere. It launched itself at me with blinding speed. I spun around, pulling up my weapon. Moving fast, I aimed the crosshairs at the zombie's chest and pulled the trigger.

'Gotcha!' I shouted. Green zombie guts sprayed everywhere.

'Nice one,' said Sophie. She was standing beside me on the roof of the abandoned building. 'Oh no! Here comes another wave!'

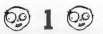

The undead creatures vaulted over the edge of the roof. There were dozens of them! Where had they all come from? Three of them sprinted straight toward me. Their zombie eyes glowed bright red. Their mouths hung open, and I could see their razor-sharp teeth glinting in the sunlight. Their arms were outstretched, their hands grasping at the air.

I loaded up and fired a couple of shots at the nearest zombies. Suddenly, everything went red. I'd been hit from behind! I crumpled to the ground.

Zombie laughter filled the air.

I flung the controller down onto the sofa, even though I knew my character would respawn. Man! I hated those guys!

'Don't rage-quit on me now!' said Sophie. She was battling the horde alone. I knew she'd never survive by herself. Sure

enough, it didn't take long; in less than a minute, the zombies were laughing again. 'We'll never get past this level,' she complained, slumping down beside me.

'Yeah. It's rigged,' I said. 'Let's watch a movie instead. How about *A Zombie Ate My Homework*?' That was my favourite zombie movie. It's about this kid who finds a baby zombie and looks after it, sort of like a pet. Except the zombie ends up following him to school one day and scaring all the kids.

'Nah,' said Sophie. 'We watched it yesterday.'

'Got any better ideas?' I asked.

'Nope,' she said.

Sophie could be annoying sometimes. But I have to put up with her because she's been my best friend ever since her parents moved to our town two years ago. Some of the kids at school think it's weird that we're friends, because she's a girl. But she can beat all of them at arm wrestling and

Me   Sophie

running, so who cares, right? She's also taller than all the other girls in our year. She's even a tiny bit taller than me, although I'm kind of short and skinny for my age. I wear my hair sticking straight up to add a couple of inches.

'OK,' I said. 'Do you wanna watch a different movie?'

'How about *American Zombie?*'

I groaned, but she ignored me and slid the DVD into the player. Old-style credits rolled up the screen as the opening music kicked in. A zombie lurched out of a house and across the street. Even though it didn't look very scary, people screamed and ran away from it.

'I can see a bit of the guy's real hair sticking out from under the wig,' said Sophie, squinting at the TV. 'And is that a zip up the back of his neck?'

'Yup!' I said. I was kind of getting into it. The thing is, I love zombie movies. Especially old zombie movies. I love new zombie movies too, although sometimes they actually are scary, unlike the ones that were made ages ago.

The zombie limped slowly after people, who hid behind cars and ran into houses. I didn't know why they bothered running; it's not like the old-style zombie could move very fast.

old-fashioned zombie   modern zombie

I yawned.

Sophie lives only a couple of blocks from me so we ride home from school together every day. Usually, we hang out at my place; I hardly ever go to her house, because Sophie's mum works all the time and Sophie's dad is a writer so he always wants us to be quiet. We're supposed to do our homework, but most of the time we do other stuff, like read comics. Reading is part of our homework anyway, so I'm only half-lying when I tell Mum we *are* doing our homework.

The zombie reached the end of the street. It looked around, then started slowly up a path toward a house. Of course it was the house where the kid who ends up killing all the zombies lived.

'Don't choose that house, zombie,' I said to the screen, even though I knew the zombie couldn't hear me. 'Choose another one. There's an old lady living next door. Go and eat her brains.'

'Nom, nom, nom,' said Sophie. That was our zombie-eating-brains noise. Sometimes we say it when we're eating ice cream or chocolate or something delicious.

Thinking about that made me hungry.

'Mum, I'm hungry!' I yelled.

'There are biscuits in the jar,' Mum shouted back from the other end of the house.

'Why do I have to do everything around

here?' I groaned. That's the problem with having parents — they're always trying to make us do things for ourselves.

'I'll get them,' said Sophie, rolling off the sofa.

I settled back and relaxed. The zombie was lumbering through the kid's house. The little kid was alone, hiding in a cupboard in his room. Didn't he know he should make a run for it before the zombie got too close? I mean, it's completely obvious that a zombie can't catch you if you're running away. But if you get cornered, you're a sitting duck!

'Here,' said Sophie, tossing me a couple of biscuits.

'Thanks,' I said.

The zombie was in the boy's room now. It was heading toward the cupboard. It lurched forward to open the door.

Suddenly, something shot past my face and landed on Sophie's back just as she bit into her biscuit. 'Nom, nom, n— AAAAGGGHHHH!'

2

Sophie screamed and leapt to her feet. She danced around, trying to pull the thing off her dress.

'Michael!' I shouted. Sure enough, my big brother leapt out from behind the sofa, laughing his head off.

'Gotcha!' he shouted, pointing at Sophie before disappearing down the hall, probably to cause trouble somewhere else. He was so annoying!

'It's OK,' I said, pulling the fluffy round

ball from Sophie's back. 'It's just a Fuzzil.' Fuzzils were the latest craze at school. People loved throwing them at each other because they stuck to your clothes and hair. They also came with removable features so you could customise them.

'I thought they were supposed to bring good luck,' said Sophie, staring at the toy in my hand. I'd heard that too, though I'd never seen anything lucky happen when a

Detention!

teacher busted you pegging a Fuzzil at someone.

She snatched it and stuffed it into her backpack. 'Well, it's just given Michael some bad luck — I'm keeping it.'

We settled down again to watch the rest of the movie, but I couldn't help checking behind us every few minutes to make sure Michael wasn't coming back. It would be just like him to creep up and leap out again, right when a zombie was going to attack someone. Even though I was eleven and he was thirteen, he acted younger than me. Sophie didn't know how lucky she was to be an only child!

In the movie, the zombie had finally found the boy hiding in the cupboard. The kid managed to escape by doing a roly-poly between the zombie's legs, then bolting out of the room. He hid again, under the dining table this time. Now the zombie was sniffing around the kitchen, getting closer and closer. The kid was shivering with fear …

'BENJAMIN ROY!' screeched a voice just behind me.

'What?!' I screamed.

I didn't mean to scream. But because I was *expecting* Michael to give me a fright, I *got* a fright.

It was only Mum this time, though. She was standing behind me, glaring at the TV. 'I thought you two were doing your homework.'

'Um … we are?' I said, which didn't sound very convincing. 'We're doing … research for an assignment.'

'Well it looks like you're watching a zombie movie to me,' said Mum. 'I don't want your grades to get any worse.'

That was totally unfair because it's not like I get bad grades. I mean, on my last report card I actually got a B!

I didn't say that though. 'Sorry, Mum,' I said. 'We were just about to start.'

REPORT CARD
BENJAMIN ROY
MATH   [D]
ENGLISH   [D]
SCIENCE   [C]
P.E.   [B] ←←←
SPELLING   [D]
BENJAMIN ROY CAN DO NO BETTER. HE DOES NOT TRY HARD ENOUGH. IN CLASS. BLAH BLAH BLAH

'It's too late now.' She sighed. 'It's getting dark.'

We all knew what that meant: it was time for Sophie to go home.

'See you later,' said Sophie, picking up her bag. 'Thanks for having me, Mrs Roy.'

'See you tomorrow, Sophie,' said Mum. She was already dishing up sausages and mashed potatoes at the dining table. 'Michael! Jeff!' she shouted. Jeff is my dad.

He works as a mechanic fixing trucks for a transport company.

I said goodbye to Sophie and we all sat down at the table. I started gobbling my food as fast as I could, so I could watch the end of the zombie movie before I went to bed.

'You're not watching the rest of that movie,' said Mum, as though she was reading my mind.

'But …' I tried not to whine but I was really disappointed. 'It's just coming up to a good part.'

'No,' she said firmly. 'I want you to do some homework first and then have a shower.'

'But I'm clean! Look!' I showed her my arm, which turned out to have a bit of dirt on it. I quickly showed her my other one instead.

'You need a shower, Ben,' said Dad. Like he could talk — he didn't look too clean himself! He always came home covered in grease and oil.

'Ben-ja-min Roy: stin-ky boy!' Michael sang, bobbing his head around as though he was dancing to music.

'Michael,' said Mum sharply.

Michael tried to look innocent, but nobody fell for it.

By the time I'd eaten dinner and had a shower and done some homework, it was time for bed. I climbed under the covers. I was still annoyed at Michael. All the kids in my class thought he was so awesome, but they didn't know what a pain he was!

Mum stuck her head in the door. 'Night, Ben,' she said, as she turned out the light and closed the door behind her.

'Night,' I said, already feeling sleepy.

I must've dropped right off, because the next thing I knew, something woke me up.

3

The room was dark and silent, but something wasn't right. The curtains were moving a little and the door was now wide open.

I started to sit up and then I saw it: something on my pillow, about an inch from my nose.

It was a zombie!

I sat bolt upright. The zombie head rolled off my pillow and fell on the floor. I jumped out of bed and turned on the

light. The head was staring
up at me from the carpet.
Its mouth gaped open and
its eyes were looking in
different directions. There
was even something that
looked like blood dribbling down its chin.

A zombie Fuzzil!

Michael strikes again, I thought, as I
picked up the Fuzzil and flung it across
the room. One day I would get my big
brother back. One day I'd be stronger and
faster than him. Then he'd be sorry!

I climbed back into bed and nodded off,
dreaming of revenge.

It seemed like only a few seconds later that
Mum was pulling open the curtains and
saying 'Rise and shine!' in that annoying
sing-song voice she used every morning.

I groaned and hid my face under the pillow. 'Just one more minute!'

I must've nodded off again and she must've got distracted, because by the time she realised I still wasn't up, it was almost time to leave for school.

'BENJAMIN ROY!' she shouted just beside my head. 'YOU ARE GOING TO BE LATE!'

That got me up! Parents could be so impatient!

Still feeling sleepy, I climbed out of bed and dragged on my clothes.

Michael was already gone. He always walked to school instead of riding his bike, because he didn't want the wind to mess up his hair. As if that would happen! He wore so much gel, a hurricane wouldn't budge it!

I went to the kitchen to get my lunchbox. There wasn't any time for breakfast.

'Can I have a coffee?' This was a question I asked Mum every morning. Not that I actually wanted a coffee. The truth was, I'd had a taste of it once at Sophie's house and we'd both thought it was disgusting. But Michael had been allowed to start drinking it a couple of months ago, so why shouldn't I?

'Will it help you ride your bike more safely?'

'No,' I guessed. 'But it might help me go faster!'

'That's what I'm afraid of!' She handed me a glass of milk which I gulped down.

'Bye, Mum!'

'Wait a minute!' Mum raced out the door after me. 'I got you a new beanie.' It was made of green material and lined with this soft fluffy  stuff that looked pretty cosy. 'It's a bit more grown-up than the last one. Put it on. It's cold today.'

'Thanks,' I said, yanking the new beanie over my ears. The last one had been a real joke. It was pale blue with a picture of a

kitten on it. On the back were the words: *Have a purrfect day!*

I know. How embarrassing, right? That's why I only wore it when it was absolutely freezing.

'Thanks,' I said again because, believe me, I was grateful.

I wheeled my bike out of the shed and took off down the street. Even though it was cold, the sun was out. It was a perfect day for the beach or skating at the park — anything other than school!

I turned into Sophie's street — her house happened to be on the way to school anyway, so we usually rode there together. Her house looked a bit different from most in our neighbourhood. The grass was

creeping out over the kerb. The fences were leaning over. But the thing that really made it stand out was the old broken-down bus parked on one side of the front yard. It had been there since they'd arrived at Seabrook two years ago. Now the tyres were flat and rust had appeared along the sides. Sophie's dad spent most of his time inside the bus, probably writing, though no one knew for sure. The windows of the bus were covered so we couldn't get a peek inside. Once, when we knew Sophie's dad was asleep, we tried to sneak in, but the door was locked.

Even from the end of the road, I could see that there was no car in Sophie's driveway, which meant that her mum had already gone to work. Sophie's mum worked at the nursing home. It was her job to play with the oldies. She would watch movies or do jigsaw puzzles with them — which didn't really sound like work to me.

I skidded up the driveway and jumped off my bike. There were three steps up to Sophie's front door, and every day I tried to leap up to the top step with my feet together. This is way harder than it sounds, especially if you keep your knees together too. I paused at the bottom of the stairs and bent my knees.

But just as I was about to jump, a hand went over my mouth.

4

My lips were clamped shut and I couldn't make a sound. Then an arm, which felt like it belonged to someone much bigger and stronger than me, went around my neck and I was dragged backward, my heels scraping along in the dirt, toward the old bus. I tried to wriggle out from underneath the arm, but my legs were sort of running the wrong way and I could hardly breathe.

My beanie fell off and landed in the mud.

The person dragging me stopped.

'Ben?'

I was released so suddenly that I almost collapsed. Sagging forward, I coughed a few times, clutching my throat.

'Are you alright, kid?'

Sophie's dad, Mr Knight, came into view. One of his meaty hands was still on my shoulder, although now he was holding me up. As usual, he was wearing one of his embarrassing aprons.

'What…?Why…?'I stammered.

'Sorry,' he said awkwardly. 'I thought you were someone else. What happened to the other hat you sometimes wear?'

'The other hat?' I said.

'You know, the blue hat. The one that says "Have a nice day" on the back.'

'"Have a purrfect day",' I said, which

was pretty dumb because it really didn't matter what the hat said.

'That's it!' cried Mr Knight, squeezing my shoulder and staring into my eyes as though he was worried I might be concussed. Which, judging from what I'd said, was probably exactly how I sounded.

'Who did you think I was?' I asked, trying to sound normal although I was still breathing like Darth Vader.

'Um … just a bad guy. Someone I don't want around here, that's all.'

'He must be really bad if you wanted to strangle him,' I said. I wasn't scared anymore — just annoyed.

Mr Knight dropped his hand from my shoulder. He looked awkward. 'Yeah, sorry about that.'

'Sorry about what, Dad?' Sophie had appeared at the front door, Michael's Fuzzil

stuck on top of her shoulder. She stared at us. 'What happened?'

Mr Knight didn't answer her. He just kept looking at me in a strange sort of way. I kept rubbing my throat, even though it was pretty much fine. As far as headlocks went, Michael's were way worse.

'Nothing,' I said to Sophie. 'I just tripped trying to jump up the steps.'

'I knew that would happen one day!' said Sophie. 'Just a tic, I'll go grab my bag.'

She reappeared a few seconds later. 'See you, Dad!' she yelled, jumping on

her bike, which was leaning against the side of the house. She never locked it up because she always said that anyone desperate enough to steal it could keep it. So far, nobody ever had. She sailed past us onto the street.

'Guess I'm a bit overprotective, sorry about that,' said Mr Knight again, leaning down and grabbing my beanie out of the dirt. He dusted it off and handed it to me. 'I'm glad you didn't mention it to Sophie.'

'No problem,' I said, taking the beanie and putting it on. I headed for my bike, keen to get out of there as quickly as possible. The guy sure was being weird!

By the time I'd reached the end of the street, Sophie was way ahead of me and pedalling hard. We always race to school. The trouble is that she usually wins, especially if she gets a head-start. I decided

to take a short-cut through Henderson Park. I could see her flying along the road just beside me. At the park entrance, I swerved between the posts and zoomed up the footpath to avoid the speed bumps on the road at the school gate. It was against school rules to ride on the footpath, especially just before the bell went when heaps of kids were arriving, but I was pretty awesome at riding my bike and I knew I wouldn't hit anyone.

Then —

'AAAAGGGHHH!'

I swerved as fast as I could, but it wasn't fast enough. The front wheel of my bike connected with someone's legs before bumping down into the gutter, while the back wheel skidded out. I fell sideways off my bike, landing on one hand and one knee. Luckily, I'd managed to slow down

enough that the fall didn't hurt too much. Sophie glided past me, looking smug.

The legs I'd hit stopped in front of me. 'What'd you do that for?'

I was about to tell him it was *his* fault for stepping out in front of me. But when I looked up from my position on the ground, I clamped my lips shut.

The kid I'd run into was called Tank. I'm not sure if that was the name he was given by his mum and dad, or if that was just the best way to describe him. Tank was big and square and hard. He was big enough to still be standing while I was sprawled on the ground.

'Ahh …' I muttered. 'Sorry, Tank. My mistake.'

'Yeah, it was your mistake,' he said, staring down at me. 'A mistake you won't make again.'

A few people had gathered around. They looked like they were hoping for a fight.

'Well, like I said,' I began, as I climbed to my feet and brushed the dirt off my knee, 'I didn't see you there, Tank.' Some of the crowd laughed, because saying you didn't see Tank was like saying you didn't see an elephant when it was standing right in front of you. 'Umm … what I mean is …'

'You sound like you're cruisin' for a bruisin',' said Tank, suddenly leaning down so his nose was only inches from mine. *Cruisin' for a bruisin'* was Tank's favourite saying. 'Are you cruisin' for a bruisin', little Benny?' he said in a high-pitched voice, like he was talking to a kid in Year One.

 34

'Fight!' someone yelled from the crowd. Then they all started chanting: 'Fight! Fight! Fight!'

Tank pulled back his fist and took aim at my face.

5

I closed my eyes and braced myself. Getting hit by Tank would be pretty much the same as getting hit by an *actual* tank. It was not going to tickle …

'What's going on here, boys?' asked a voice.

I opened my eyes. Mr Crumpet, the Chemistry teacher, was staring down at us. I breathed a sigh of relief. Tank wouldn't dare punch me in front of a teacher, even though Mr Crumpet was probably the softest teacher in the school.

'Umm,' said Tank, thinking fast. Or at least *trying* to think fast. 'Umm …'

I had to admit, it *was* pretty hard to think around Mr Crumpet. The man was kind of weird. I mean, it's not every day you see someone wandering around with a raven on their shoulder!

Mr Crumpet had found the bird when he was just a chick. He called him Corvus and kept him as a pet. Corvus wore a little hood over his eyes, so he wouldn't fly away.

Now the bird turned his head toward the sound of our voices and made a soft clicking noise with his beak.

'It looks like Ben fell off his bike,' said Mr Crumpet, 'and you were helping him back onto his feet. Is that what happened, Tank?'

Tank nodded slowly, staring at the bird.

37

'Yeah,' he said. 'That's exactly what happened.'

I nodded too. It was such a relief not to get punched in the face by Tank, I would have agreed to anything. 'I'm OK. Thanks, Tank, for your … help.'

Tank glared at me and disappeared into the crowd.

'Looks like you've grazed your knee,' said Mr Crumpet, peering at my leg, where a drop of blood was running down my shin. 'It might be a good idea to go and give that a wash before class starts.'

'Sure, Mr Crumpet,' I said.

Mr Crumpet never *told* us to do anything. He never even made us do homework! Instead, he just 'suggested' it would be 'in our best interests' to do things, like revise around exam time. Funnily enough, everyone worked just as hard in his class as

they did in any other class. Maybe it was because Mr Crumpet seemed so gentle, none of us wanted to disappoint him.

I wheeled my bike through the school gates. Of course Sophie was just on the other side of them, looking pleased with herself.

'I won!' she said, pulling her bike in beside mine. The Fuzzil was still stuck on her shoulder.

'Yeah, whatever,' I said. How could she just ride right past me when I'd fallen off my bike? And where was she when I was attacked by the school bully? Some friend! I sped up and pushed my way through the crowd.

'What's the matter? It didn't seem like the fall hurt that much,' she said, running to keep up with me.

I didn't answer. If she couldn't figure it out, why should I tell her? Angrily, I shoved

my front tyre into the bike rack and wound my bike lock around the wheel.

'Ben!' She dropped her bike on the grass and stood with her hands on her hips. 'What's wrong?'

'Tank nearly punched my lights out!' I said.

'What?' She looked stunned, but I didn't buy it. 'When?'

'Just now.' I was so mad, I was almost shouting. 'After I fell off my bike!'

'Are you OK …?'

I ignored her. It was obvious she didn't care! I dodged around her and lost her among the crowd. Maybe washing my knee was a good idea; that way she wouldn't be able to follow me into the boys' toilets.

The bell rang as I walked through the school doors. The hallway was filled with

kids, some taking things out of their lockers, some chatting as they made their way to class. A few said hello to me, but I pretended not to hear them as I made a beeline for the boys' toilets, which were down the end of another smaller, less crowded hallway, opposite an old staircase. The staircase was blocked off with a rope, which had a little sign dangling over it:

I think this was meant to show people the stairs were steep and dangerous, but someone had drawn on it with a black marker. Now the sign looked like this:

If it hadn't been for the sign, I would never have even noticed that one of the panels, which blocked off the space under the stairs, was loose. I stopped to inspect it. It wasn't loose; it was *open*. What seemed to be a bit of ordinary wall panelling was actually a door. It reminded me of one of my favourite video games, *Return of the Infected*. Zombies would jump out from hidden doorways when you least expected it. Could zombies be lurking here too?

I looked around. The hallway was now empty. I pulled the door open further.

Inside was a small room. The floor was cluttered with stuff: stacks of buckets, boxes of rags, vacuum cleaners and other machines. Mops were leant up against one corner. A shelf, with fancy carved knobs at either end, ran along the length of one wall. It was piled high with cleaning products.

This must be the janitor's storeroom. It made sense that they would want this stuff near the toilets, but they wouldn't want the kids to know where it was kept. People would come in and trash it! I imagined Tank in here, emptying the bottles of detergent on the floor and unravelling the rolls of toilet paper. He'd make a real mess of the place if he knew about it. I stepped back, pulling the door shut. I felt a bit disappointed because, for some reason, I thought I had discovered a secret room.

But just as the weird door-disguised-as-a-panel was swinging shut, I saw something: a movement. I pushed the door open again and there it was, right in front of me — a gaping hole in the wall.

6

The opening was about the size and shape of a door, and as black as the mouth of a cave. A slight wind blew up out of it. The air smelt old and stale.

For a few seconds I stood still, staring into the pitch-black hole. Where had it suddenly appeared from? I'm pretty sure my mouth was gaping too, because it's not very often that a portal into the unknown opens up before your eyes. I decided I should get a closer look. Maybe I'd found a secret zombie crypt after all!

I put my bag down and began to pick

my way carefully between a box of rags and a big, old machine that I guessed was used to polish the floor.

Suddenly, there was a sound behind me. I must've been kind of jumpy 'cause I spun around real quick. My leg hit the floor-polisher and, as I fell, I tried to grab the wooden shelf.

'WHAT DO YOU THINK YOU ARE DOING?' boomed a voice.

I looked up from where I was sprawled on the floor. Standing in the hallway was Mr Slender.

Mr Slender, the Maths teacher, was tall and thin and sharp. Unlike old Crumpet, whenever Mr Slender opened his mouth it was to give an order or to tell

someone off. Sometimes, if he was really angry, he threw bits of chalk at people. Everyone was petrified of him.

'Ummm,' I said, wondering why, out of all the teachers in school, it had to be Slender who caught me. I must've been in shock because I added, 'That just opened.' I pointed behind me at the back wall of the cupboard.

'What just opened?' said Mr Slender, glaring at me.

I glanced around. The hole was gone. There was just a solid wall.

'It was just there,' I said, still pointing. What had happened? Where had it gone?

'Hmmm,' said Mr Slender. 'Your knee's bleeding. Did you fall off your bike?'

I was so stunned, I could barely register what he was saying. 'There was a hole in the wall. Sort of like a doorway.'

'I'm sure there was,' said Mr Slender in a tone that made it clear he didn't believe me. 'Now did you fall off your bike or not?'

'Yeah, but I'm OK.' I stared back where the hole had been. 'It's just that this hole … it wasn't there, and then it appeared.'

'You sound confused.' Mr Slender peered at me. 'Did you hit your head in the fall?'

'Yeah — I mean no.' I suddenly *felt* confused.

'There is no hole. Look.' He gestured toward the wall. 'And as for things that appear out of nowhere, well, I've never heard anything stupider in my life. Now I think you'd better go wash your knee, then head straight to class. And I want to see you in my classroom after school so you can catch up on all the work you've already missed.'

Detention! That was so unfair! People always arrived late to the first class of the day, so it's not like I would have missed anything important!

'Off you go,' snapped Mr Slender. 'This storeroom is out of bounds. If I catch you in here again, it'll be detention for a week.'

I shot one more look at the wall, then grabbed my bag off the floor. I walked past Mr Slender into the toilets and gave my knee a quick rinse under the tap. The water was icy cold, but I hardly felt it.

Outside the bathroom, the hallway was completely deserted — except for Slender, who stood with his arms folded in front of the janitor's storeroom. Now the door was shut, the panel blended in so well with the ones alongside it that it took me a second to work out which one had opened. I headed toward my English class in a state

of disbelief. What had I just seen? Had a secret passageway really just opened up under the stairs? And if there was a secret passageway, where did it lead?

7

By lunchtime, I'd simmered down a bit. I was still pretty angry at Sophie, but I really wanted to tell her about what I'd discovered. Still, I wasn't going to let her off the hook that easily. During English I'd sat at the front while she went straight to our usual spot at the back of the room. All the way through class, she kept throwing notes at me:

I didn't see Tank hit you!

Well if you're going to be such an idiot, I'll eat lunch with Sarah!

guess who!

Sarah was the only girl in our year who Sophie occasionally hung out with. Sarah spent most of her time in the library, so 'hanging out' with her meant sitting beside her, reading a book. Not exactly my idea of fun.

I wrote a note and threw it back at her.

During lunch I hung around the hallway entrance alone, watching the janitor's storeroom. I was waiting for the hallway to clear; I didn't want anyone nearby while I was checking out the storeroom again. If there was a secret passageway, I wanted to be the first to explore it.

It wasn't until the bell rang, and the last classroom door banged shut, that the corridor was empty. But just as I was about

to step into the hallway, Mr Slender appeared again.

'Still hanging around out here?' he asked, striding toward me.

'I was just getting some books out of my locker,' I lied, relieved I happened to be standing near it. I opened my locker door and rummaged around inside, waiting for him to leave.

He stood there watching me until I'd grabbed a couple of books and closed the door again.

'Off you go,' he said, still glaring at me. 'And don't forget: detention in my room after school.'

I had no choice. I had to go to class.

The rest of the afternoon dragged. By the time we were in History, our last class of the day, I was sick of being angry at Sophie. I threw her a note:

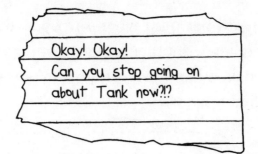

She threw one back:

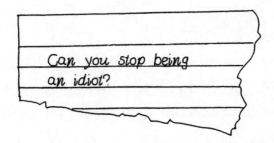

I wrote:

I heard her gasp when she opened it. A minute later, another tiny wad of paper hit my back. When the teacher wasn't looking, I picked it up.

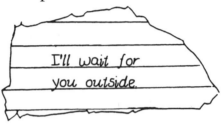

I'll wait for you outside.

Detention was always held in Mr Slender's room. Nobody knew why he always supervised detention, but I'm pretty sure it was because he enjoyed watching people suffer.

I sat at the back of the room, watching the hands of the clock inching around, and secretly reading the emergency zombie comic I kept in my bag. It was an old copy of *Worm Eaten,* which was one of my all-time favourites. I was supposed to be doing

my homework, but, really, what was the point? I mean, it's not like I'd be doing my homework at home if I was there!

Mr Slender sat at the front of the room, watching us from under his eyelids. Occasionally, some kid would think he was asleep and whisper to the person beside them. These kids had obviously never been in detention before. They didn't know that with Mr Slender, if you made one false move, you got a bit of chalk thrown at your head. Or, if you were really unlucky, the duster.

Finally, the clock struck four. Just to be extra mean, Mr Slender pretended to keep sleeping. At five past four, he opened his eyes.

'I hope never to see any of you in here again,' he said, which was the line he always used at the end of detention.

I rushed out as fast as I could. Sophie

was sitting on the floor near the lockers. She stood up as I walked over to her, while the other kids ran past me to freedom.

'How come you had detention?' she asked.

'Long story,' I said. 'I think it would be easier if I just showed you.'

I glanced around. The place looked deserted. I grabbed Sophie's arm and pulled her into the smaller hallway, toward the old staircase.

'Where are we going?' she asked.

'You'll see,' I said.

We stopped outside the toilets.

'You're not going to make me go into the boys' loos, are you?' She looked around as I fiddled with the panel that opened to the janitor's storeroom.

I was worried someone would come down the hallway and see us. I could

pretend I was coming out of the toilets, but Sophie couldn't. The girls' bathroom was in a completely different part of the building.

'You wait in here,' I said, opening the door to the boys' toilets and pushing her inside. 'It'll look suspicious if anyone sees you down here.'

'I can't go in there!'

'Don't worry,' I told her. 'No one will know.'

Sophie started to say something, then she caught sight of a urinal. 'Yuck! Is that what I think it is?'

I nodded. 'Yup.'

'But … but … everyone can see you! That's disgusting!'

I left Sophie staring in horror at the urinal while I

slipped back out into the hallway. I searched around the panel for a while before I found a tiny catch on one side. The metal was stiff, but finally it clicked beneath my finger. The door creaked open.

I poked my head back into the toilets. 'C'mon,' I said to Sophie.

She looked happy to be getting out of there.

Sophie followed me into the hallway, and looked at the open panel in surprise.

'I didn't even know this was here,' she said.

'Me neither,' I said. 'But that's not the really weird thing. Check this out.' I stepped inside the cupboard and began poking around the back wall. There had to be a way to make it open again.

'It kind of stinks in here,' said Sophie. 'What are you looking for anyway?'

'When I was going to the toilets to wash my knee this morning, I found …' I paused and swallowed hard. 'I found a secret doorway.'

'Yeah. It leads to this janitor's storeroom. Can we go?'

'Not this doorway. Another one. It's here somewhere.' I felt along the wall.

'What do you mean? I can't see anything.'

'I know,' I told her. 'It's a *secret* doorway. It opened when I was standing there, right where you are.'

Sophie looked around at the piles of soap and toilet paper.

'Maybe I bumped something accidentally, a button or a lever,' I said, running my hand over another wall.

'Yeah. Or maybe you imagined it.' Sophie was staring at me like I'd gone mad. 'Do you know how weird this sounds?'

'It was the wooden knob,' I said suddenly. 'I tripped and grabbed the knob on the end of the shelf as I fell. That seemed to close the door — maybe it will open it too.'

I raised my hand toward the carved piece of wood, and wrapped my fingers around the knob. The wood felt smooth beneath my skin. I twisted.

8

But the secret door didn't open.

I twisted my hand the other way. I pulled it forward, pushed it backward and side to side. Still nothing. Standing on tiptoes, I peered at the knob.

'It's from the old library,' Sophie explained. 'I recognise the shelf. They installed new ones a couple of years ago, just after we moved here. All the old wooden shelves were taken away. I guess they decided to use some of them around the school.'

How fascinating, I thought sarcastically. I was pretty sure I could have figured that

out for myself, if I ever went into the library.

I didn't say that though. I didn't want Sophie to get mad at me again.

'I don't know why it isn't working,' I said instead. I picked my way through the clutter over to where the door had appeared. It still looked like a completely normal wall, made of old planks. In fact, it looked like the last wall in the world where a secret door might be hidden.

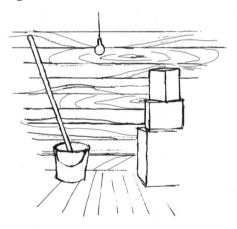

'Where were you standing when you saw it?' asked Sophie.

'Here.' I stepped back outside the door. 'I saw it open right over *there*.'

Sophie stood behind me, staring at the wall.

'So you were here, in the hallway?'

'Yup. The door was swinging shut when I saw something move. So I pushed the door back open again and that's when I saw it.'

'Maybe it was a mop falling over,' said Sophie, nodding toward the wooden handles standing up in one corner, 'and it just *looked* like something opening.'

'It wasn't a mop.'

'A broom?'

'It wasn't a broom,' I said. I was starting to feel annoyed. I twisted the knob again. Nothing happened. I pushed it down. Then

up. I looked under the shelf at the wooden brackets that held it in place. If only the door would open — that would show her!

'Why didn't you get closer? Why didn't you go inside the cupboard?' asked Sophie.

'I was going to,' I snapped. 'But I tripped.'

'Did you see it shut?'

'Yes! No … I don't know. Slender was there, and when I looked back the door had closed.'

'Did Slender see it?'

'I don't think so. He said it sounded like I hit my head when I fell off my bike.'

'Maybe you did,' said Sophie.

I closed my eyes and took a deep breath. Did she *practise* being annoying?

tap tap

'I've got to go,' she added. 'I'm already late.'

'Fine,' I said, not looking at her.

'Why don't you come over to my place? Mum just got me *Zombie Attack 3*. I haven't even opened it yet.'

'Awesome!' I breathed before I could stop myself. Maybe Sophie wasn't *that* annoying after all! *Zombie Attack 3* was the latest video game — all the kids were talking about it. I really wanted to get it, but there was no way I could afford it, even if I saved every cent of my pocket money for the next three years.

We played for an hour before we managed to get through the first level without being eaten by the horde of hungry zombies. It wasn't until Mr Knight told Sophie that she needed to turn it off soon, because dinner

was nearly ready, that I realised it was almost completely dark outside. I wanted to stay and keep playing, but I knew Mum would be annoyed if I didn't get home soon.

'Mum's working late this week,' Sophie explained, as she firebombed a few zombies that were trailing behind the others, 'so Dad's cooking.' She made a grossed-out face and I guessed Mr Knight's cooking wasn't great.

I headed for the door. 'Maybe we can look for the secret door again tomorrow.'

She wrinkled up her nose. 'I don't want to go into the boys' toilet again. It's so gross.'

'You could wait outside in the corridor while I look for it,' I suggested.

'Maybe,' said Sophie, without taking her eyes off the screen. 'Bye.'

'See you.' I slung my bag onto my back and walked out into the hallway.

'Ben.' Mr Knight appeared at the kitchen door. He was holding a pair of tongs and still wearing that flowery apron over his clothes. I pretended not to notice. He dipped his head toward the kitchen. 'Just come in here for a second.'

I glanced back at Sophie. She was too busy battling the zombies to notice.

In the kitchen, Mr Knight was frying something in a pan. It looked like some sort of vegetable sludge mixed with brown sauce. No wonder Sophie hated his cooking. He poked at a mushroom with his wooden spoon. 'I heard you talking about a secret door at school.'

I blinked. Had he been spying on us?

I must've looked surprised because he quickly added, 'I just caught it as I was walking past.'

'Um … I found this weird hidden door. It leads into the janitor's storeroom.'

'I know the one,' said Mr Knight casually, looking back at the pan. 'The storeroom has been there ever since the school was used as a hospital.'

I nodded politely. Everyone knew that Seabrook High used to be a hospital ages ago.

'It's not really a secret,' he added. 'It was just built to blend in with the wall.'

'Inside the cupboard is another door. That's the secret one,' I blurted out.

'Ahhh!' said Mr Knight knowingly. 'They must've blocked off part of the cupboard for a new hot-water system. A wise move. They probably don't want the kids to know where it is just in case someone vandalises it.'

I stared at him. Did he really think I would believe that?

'It might not be a good idea to poke around in there — it could be dangerous,' he continued.

'OK,' I said.

'And I don't want you or Sophie to get into trouble.' He glanced at me.

'OK,' I said again, wondering why he was making such a big deal about this. Did he know something about the secret door? Why was he so keen for me to stay away from it?

'You better head home before your mum gets worried,' he added.

My cue to exit. 'Bye, Mr Knight.'

Outside, I picked up my bike from where I'd dumped it on the front lawn and headed for the road. Mr Knight sure was acting strangely. First he'd grabbed me around the neck and then he'd spied on us. Since he seemed so interested in what I was doing, maybe it was time I found out a bit more about him! As I walked past the old bus, I stopped and glanced around; the street was deserted. From where I stood, I could hear Mr Knight rattling around inside the kitchen. I lowered my bike onto the grass and crept behind the vehicle. The bus was identical to the one in *Revenge of the Brain Munchers*. About halfway through the movie, zombies have the good guys cornered inside it, but just as the horde of

undead break down the door, the hero realises the back window of the bus pops out and they all escape in the nick of time.

I gazed up at the back window of Mr Knight's bus; a pair of hinges was attached above it and there was a handle jutting out from underneath. It was obviously an escape hatch in case the bus was in an accident. Who knew breaking into a bus would be so easy? And to think Mum always said I'd learn nothing useful from watching zombie movies!

I climbed onto the back bumper and turned the handle. There was a sharp click and the window swung out. I must've been nervous 'cause, even though the night air was cool, sweat ran down my neck. Trying to move quietly, I slipped into the bus.

I haven't been in that many buses in my time; in fact I've only ridden in the big old

coaches the school uses during sports competitions. Not that I'm really into sports, but you just about have to be at death's door before they'll let you get out of it.

'Don't worry, we've only signed you up for shot put and long jump.'

Anyway, the point is that I'm not much of an expert when it comes to buses. But climbing through that window, even I knew enough to realise that this was no ordinary bus.

Instead of seats, the bus contained what looked like an office. There was a comfy-looking chair in front of a desk. A couple of old filing cabinets with overflowing drawers stood against one wall. Beside these was a bookcase crammed with newspapers.

Weirdest of all, every window in the bus had been covered with corkboards. Pinned to these were all sorts of things: newspaper clippings, maps, photos. There were also some old pictures of zombies scattered among the regular photos, which was kind of strange 'cause I didn't know Mr Knight was into zombies. Notes were scribbled all over them, in messy handwriting.

I walked further into the bus. Behind the desk was a big map. I peered at it; it wasn't really a map at all. It was actually a plan of a building. And not just any building.

In front of me was a plan of Seabrook High.

I swallowed hard. Why would Mr Knight have a plan of the school?

I looked closely; there was the front door that led into the main hallway. There were the classrooms branching off to the left and right. There was the small hallway that led to the boys' toilets. And there — I could hardly breathe — there was the staircase where I'd found the hidden storeroom. *And it was marked with a red cross.*

I gaped. Why would Mr Knight mark the spot with a red cross if it was only an old storeroom?

My eyes leapt to another red cross drawn on the plan. This one was in a different part of the building. It only took me a second to realise that it was positioned over the lines that marked one of the classroom

cupboards. The cupboard inside Mr Slender's room.

'Ben!'

I spun around. Mr Knight was standing at the door of the bus, clutching a huge knife in his hand.

9

'Did I startle you?' he said. 'Here, your mum's on the phone.' Mr Knight handed me the telephone, which I hadn't noticed he was holding in his other hand. I guess I was distracted by the enormous knife!

'Hello?' I croaked.

'Ben! Where are you? You know the rules!' Mum sounded annoyed.

'Sorry, Mum, I'm still at Sophie's house,' I said. I almost added, *I'm in the bus with Mr Knight and he has a huge knife!* But I didn't.

'I know you're at Sophie's,' said Mum. 'I was just talking to Gerald. You should be home by now.'

'I'm on my way. Bye.' I handed the phone back to Mr Knight and headed for the door. Mr Knight leant to the side so I could squeeze past him. As I rushed down the steps, I heard his voice behind me.

'Sorry, Lynn, I thought he'd already gone. No problem. He's on his way now. See …'

By then I was out of earshot.

I jumped on my bike and pedalled as fast as I could. My mind was racing. Any doubts that I had seen a secret doorway open inside the janitor's storeroom were gone. And why did Mr Knight have a copy of the school's plan pinned to his wall?

I tore home. The night air was cold against my face, but I hardly noticed. The streets looked different: the yards were full of shadows and the houses seemed to watch me with their blank, dark windows.

It wasn't far to my house, but it seemed to take longer than usual. Finally, I turned into our driveway and glided into the back yard. The shed door was open and, although it was pitch black inside, I rode in and skidded to a stop. I'd done it so many times, I could've done it blindfolded.

I jumped off my bike and headed for the back door. Inside, everyone was already eating dinner.

'Ben,' said Dad, 'you're late.'

'Sorry,' I said, dumping my bag on the sofa. 'Got a flat tyre on the way back from Sophie's house.'

Mum raised her eyebrows. 'I thought you were still *at* Sophie's house when I rang a couple of minutes ago. Or was I talking to a ghost?'

'Oh yeah.' What a rookie mistake! I guess I was still a bit shaky from the shock of

seeing Mr Knight in the bus with that knife. Man! That totally freaked me out!

Dad pointed with his fork at my chair. 'Sit.'

I sat down and stared at my plate.

'And I don't want to hear any complaints about dinner,' Mum added.

I eyed the Brussels sprouts piled on one side of my plate. 'Mmmm! Meatloaf and veggies. This looks great!' I stabbed one of the sprouts with my fork and put the whole thing in my mouth. Trying not to gag, I chewed as fast as I could.

'yum'

'Ben got detention today,' Michael said in a happy voice. He smiled across the table at me.

Mum put down her fork. 'How come?'

I glared at Michael. 'Dno, glubolem…' I tried to speak, but I still had a mouth full of Brussels sprouts.

'He was beating up another kid,' said Michael.

'WHAT!' screamed Mum.

I almost choked on the sprout. Finally, I managed to swallow it. 'I was not! I was late to class, that's all.'

'Ooohh!' said Michael. 'So you didn't get detention for the fight, you got it for *another* thing!'

'What fight?' Mum asked.

'There was no fight!' I said angrily. 'I was late to class and Mr Slender gave me a detention. It's no big deal.'

'So it wasn't you who picked a fight with Tank?' asked Michael. 'It was some *other* kid called Benjamin Roy who happens to go to our school and who looks *exactly* like you?'

'Why were you late to class?' asked Dad.

'I was in the toilets. I wasn't … feeling very well,' I said.

'You mean you were in the toilets crying after Tank beat you up,' said Michael. Bits of meatloaf sprayed out of his mouth.

'Michael!' said Mum crossly. 'Don't speak with your mouth full.'

'Who's Tank?' asked Dad.

'Just a kid,' I said. 'Anyway, the good news is that I did all my homework while I was in detention, so I don't have any left to finish tonight.' Ha ha! Take that, Michael!

'Did you?' Mum looked completely stunned.

'Yup! And I got a head-start on my history assignment.' Okay, so that wasn't exactly true either, but I was going to start the assignment soon so it wouldn't be a lie for long.

'Well, that's very good, Ben.' Mum picked up her fork again. 'I always say: "when life gives you lemons, make lemonade".'

I'm pretty sure I had never heard Mum say that before, but I wasn't about to burst her bubble, so I just nodded. 'And I think I'll have an early night tonight. Got a big science test tomorrow.'

'Great idea!' Mum looked like she was going to explode with happiness.

'I heard Tank's pretty ticked off about this morning,' said Michael.

'That'll be twenty cents into the swearing jar, Michael!' Mum's idea of swearing started at words like 'darn' and 'jeez', so 'ticked off' was hardcore cussing to her.

'I'm just saying Ben had better watch his back.' Michael seemed really annoyed. He shoved the last bit of his meatloaf into his mouth and chewed hard.

'You're his big brother. You should be looking out for him,' Dad said.

'It's OK, Dad,' I said in my bravest voice. 'I'm used to looking after myself.'

Round one of the night to me.

I was pretty quiet for the rest of dinner. I was too busy coming up with a plan to talk. I had to get into the cupboard in Mr Slender's room somehow — but first I needed supplies.

After dinner, I waited until Dad was busy with the washing-up and Mum was talking on the phone in her bedroom. I could hear the shower running so I guessed Michael was in the bathroom.

I yawned and stretched. 'Think I might head off to bed. Got a big day tomorrow.'

Dad was whistling along to the radio, so I don't think he even noticed.

I slipped down the hallway. Steam was creeping out from under the bathroom door. It looked just like the mist that always appears in old zombie movies, which kind of suited my mission. Michael always spent ages in the shower — not that it made him

smell any better — so I knew he wouldn't interrupt me anytime soon. The last thing I needed was someone asking awkward questions about what I was doing!

I held my breath and sneaked into the laundry. Mum always adds this smelly stuff to the washing machine so the whole room stinks like flowers. It was a relief when I opened the back door and stepped outside. I crept past the washing line and into the shed, then I felt around on the bench for the torch Dad always keeps there for when the power goes off. I pressed my palm over the end of it and switched it on. Then I arranged my fingers so that just enough light shone through for me to see what I was doing.

Against the wall was an old cupboard where Dad kept what he called 'emergency supplies'. We'd never had an emergency

worse than the water getting turned off for an hour or two, so I'm not sure what sort of thing he had in mind. Inside the cupboard I found some spare batteries for the torch and on one of the shelves was a coil of rope, but when I tried to lift it, I almost fell over — it was too big and heavy to be of any use to me. There wasn't much else in the cupboard except for an old radio and a fire extinguisher. So much for Dad's ideas about surviving an emergency. We wouldn't last five minutes in a zombie apocalypse! I slipped out of the shed with the torch and batteries.

Back inside the house, Michael was still in the shower. Hopefully, he would use up all the hot water so I wouldn't have to have one.

Feeling relieved I'd made it back inside without anyone noticing I'd gone, I went into my bedroom. And almost screamed.

 88

10

All my soft toys were hanging around the edge of my bed from bits of string. It was so creepy!

Now I don't have that many soft toys. Mostly they're from when I was little. I got them as gifts so I can't really get rid of them

without offending a lot of people. Anyway, they're usually lined up along my pillow during the day and I throw them onto the floor at night.

I stared at them. It was easy to guess who had done it. 'MICHAEL!'

Mum's head appeared around the doorway. 'What's the matter?'

'Look what he did!'

'Hmmm.' She didn't look all that annoyed. In fact, I think she actually smiled a bit. 'Michael!'

'Yes, beloved Mother?' Michael wandered in. He had a towel wrapped around his waist and his eyebrows were up in their usual 'innocent' expression.

Mum pointed at my bed. 'Did you do this?'

Michael slapped his hands

to his cheeks. 'Why, those poor little toys!'

'Michael …' said Mum in her warning tone.

'Mother, I'm shocked that you would accuse me of this terrible crime!'

Mum was definitely trying not to smile. How did he always get away with this stuff? 'You can help take them down. Go and get some scissors.'

'Maybe they need to be resuscitated,' said Michael. 'Stand back! I shall give them mouth-to-mouth.' He opened his mouth like a vampire and walked toward the bed. 'Come here, little teddies! This won't hurt a bit!'

'Michael!' Mum was laughing now! *Openly laughing!*

'Get out!' I pushed him back toward the door. 'Never come into my room again! Never!'

It took me ages to untie them, but finally all the toys were in a pile beside my bed. I bundled up the string and threw it in my bin. I was going to toss it into Michael's room and let him clean it up, but I knew he'd probably tell Mum and I'd have to pick it up *all over again*! He was so spoilt!

I replaced the batteries in the torch with fresh ones and put it in my backpack, then pulled on my PJs and climbed into bed. I was starting to get nervous about tomorrow. What if the plan didn't work? What if I got caught? The more I thought about it, the more worried I became.

'BENJAMIN!' screamed Mum right beside my head. 'You are going to be late for school!'

I groaned and tried to open my eyes. Surely it couldn't be morning yet? I couldn't even remember going to sleep!

I rolled out of bed and found the clothes I'd worn yesterday in a heap on the floor. They were clean enough — only a few stains here and there — so I pulled them on.

Mum eyed me suspiciously as I walked into the kitchen. 'Isn't that what you were wearing yesterday?'

'Yup,' I said. 'Just trying to cut down on the washing.'

'Hmmmm,' said Mum, raising an eyebrow.

I gobbled down a piece of toast and sculled a glass of milk. 'Can I have a coffee?'

'No,' said Mum. 'Here's your lunch.'

I shoved the lunchbox in my bag, keeping my back to her so she wouldn't see the

torch. Trying to act casually, I headed for the door.

'Ben?' she called, just when I thought I'd got away with it. 'Come back here for a second.'

My heart sank. What had given me away?

I trooped back into the kitchen. 'Yeah?'

Mum leant down. 'Good luck on your science test today,' she said and planted a kiss on my forehead.

'Thanks, Mum.' I felt so relieved, I didn't even mind that she'd kissed me! I also felt a bit guilty. Technically, there *was* a science test, but we took one every week so it was no big deal. It's not like I'd ever study for it or anything.

Outside it was warm and sunny, but for once I actually wanted to go to school. On

the way to Sophie's house I pulled a few wheelies and did some bunny-hops. I'm already pretty good at doing tricks on my bike, but you can never have too much practice, right? I turned into her street and did a massive skid as I pulled up outside her house. Even Sophie's parents would have been impressed by that one!

Sophie was already waiting for me on the front steps. The Fuzzil was stuck to her shoulder again. She jumped up and grabbed her bike from where it was leaning against the house. But instead of getting on it, she walked it down to the end of the driveway.

'What happened last night?' she asked before she'd even reached me.

'What do you mean? Oh, with your dad?'

'Yeah, he said he caught you in the bus. He said we weren't allowed in there and

then he went out and put a lock on the back window. What were you doing?'

I glanced across at the bus. Sure enough, there was a chain with a big padlock wrapped around the handle on the back window. That guy sure didn't waste any time!

Suddenly, I wanted to get out of there.

'I'll tell you on the way,' I said, pulling my bike into a U-turn. We rode to the park in silence.

Henderson Park had all the usual stuff: swings, a merry-go-round, a slide. There was even a flying-fox. We pulled up beside the swings and jumped off our bikes. I took an old wooden swing while Sophie sat on one of the new plastic ones. That's the good thing about being best friends: sometimes you do things without having to talk about it. You just know what to do.

We didn't swing much as I explained what had happened last night. When I got to the bit about the photos and maps, she wrinkled up her nose and said, 'That's weird!'

'Yeah,' I said. 'It was definitely creepy.'

'And you're sure it was a map of our school?' she asked.

'Positive. And when I looked at the map, I saw the janitor's storeroom was marked with a red cross. So was the cupboard in Mr Slender's classroom. What do you think that could mean?'

But Sophie didn't answer the question. Instead she dug the toes of her shoes into the sand. 'It's kind of strange that these things keep happening to you, don't you think?'

'What do you mean?' I asked.

'Well,' she said as she stared at something behind me, 'it's just weird that only *you* see these things. First there was the secret door under the stairs and now this. Dad's a writer, so maybe he has stuff in his office that isn't normal.'

'Pictures of zombies? Maps of our school?'

'Yeah. So you say.'

'It's true! Why don't you look for yourself?' I was getting mad now. What was the point of having a best friend if they didn't believe you? 'Oh hang on a minute, you can't 'cause it's locked! Why

does he keep people out if he's got nothing to hide?'

'I don't know.' Now Sophie sounded upset. 'Maybe it's just private stuff. My dad's not a bad person.' Suddenly, she jumped off the swing and ran over to her bike. She threw her leg over it and in a couple of seconds she was riding out of the park.

'Fine,' I said out loud, even though no one was listening. I didn't need her to believe me! I knew what I saw and I knew what I was going to do. Now, I'd have to do it alone.

11

I rode the rest of the way to school. The bell was ringing as I pulled up at the bike racks, which left me with just enough time to dump my bag in my locker and head off to my first class. On the way, I took a detour past Mr Slender's room to check his timetable. I was hoping that Mr Slender would have a timeslot today when he wasn't teaching. If I knew when he'd be in the staffroom, I knew when I could sneak into his cupboard.

The timetable was stuck to his door. It seemed as though he had classes all day except for … Suddenly, the door opened and,

instead of looking at the timetable, I was staring at the front of Mr Slender's suit.

'Yes?' he said, glaring at me.

'Ummm.' I straightened up. 'I was just checking the time of … my class.'

Mr Slender's eyes gleamed like lumps of ice. 'Don't you know it yet? Might I point out that it is almost the end of term?'

'Ummmm,' I said.

'Do my classes not capture your attention? Are they not *memorable* enough? Do I have to do handstands or perform cartwheels for you?'

'No?' I guessed.

'Are you *quite* certain?' He swooped down so we were eyeball to eyeball.

'Umm … yes.' I tried to sound more confident.

'Good.' He straightened back up, adjusting the front of his jacket. Then he

fiddled with the cuffs of his sleeves before glancing back down at me. 'Are you still here?'

I had no choice. Slowly, I turned away.

I was pretty sure the timetable said Mr Slender had two empty periods after lunch, but I wanted another quick look to be absolutely certain. I'd have to check it again during morning tea or lunch.

My first class was a double period of English. When I arrived, everyone was already sitting at their desks. Sophie was there, of course, but she wasn't in our usual spot at the back. Instead she was sitting toward the front between Sarah and this kid called Jimmy Cartwright. Jimmy was always boasting about how he was going to be a professional bike rider when he finished school. Most weekends, he practised with his BMX down at the skate bowl.

Sure, he could pull a few tricks, but he wasn't *that* great. If you asked me, the guy was a bit of a show-off.

I walked to my desk. Sophie made a big deal about whispering to Jimmy as I went past, but I pretended I didn't care. If she wanted to sit between Silent and Show-off, that was her business!

In English, we were studying a book called *The Astounding Art of Punctuation!*. Whoever wrote it was the biggest liar on earth because, believe me, the only thing astounding about punctuation is how incredibly boring it is.

Our teacher, Miss Mackenzie, droned on and on about putting commas in, the, right, places, and the correct use of exclamation marks and question marks. Honestly? What was the point! It was as much as I could do not to fall asleep.

Finally, the bell rang.

The worst thing about sitting up the back of the room is that everyone else gets out the door first. Today was no different; I tried to push my way through the crush, but by the time I got out of the room, Sophie had disappeared. It was so frustrating! Sure, I was mad at her, but I really wanted to talk to her about my plan!

During morning tea, I ate a couple of biscuits but I must've been getting nervous 'cause my mouth was all dry and I could hardly swallow them. I had to have a big drink of water at the bubbler just to get them down! Then the bell rang again and I had to hurry into Science. Today we had the test I'd told Mum about. Luckily, it was pretty easy and I got through most of it OK.

Science Mini test – pre-historic times

Name these fossils.

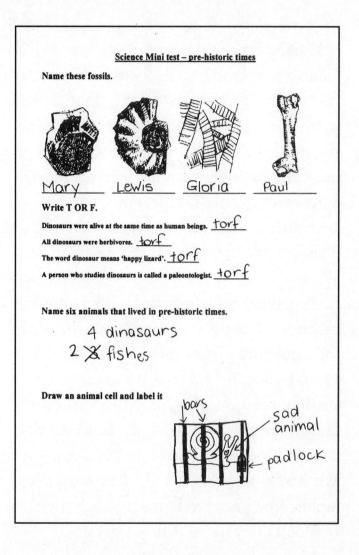

Mary   Lewis   Gloria   Paul

Write T OR F.

Dinosaurs were alive at the same time as human beings. torf

All dinosaurs were herbivores. torf

The word dinosaur means 'happy lizard'. torf

A person who studies dinosaurs is called a paleontologist. torf

Name six animals that lived in pre-historic times.

4 dinasaurs
2 ~~X~~ fishes

Draw an animal cell and label it

bars

sad animal

padlock

During lunch, I hung around outside Mr Slender's room. I didn't dare check the timetable again, because the door to his room was open and I could see him sitting there at his desk. There was no way I could get close enough without him seeing me. There was nothing to do but wait, and go over the plan in my head again and again. That's when I really started freaking out. What if it all went wrong? What if I got stuck inside the cupboard overnight? By morning, I might have peed myself! When the bell finally rang at the end of lunch, I had broken into a cold sweat.

'Ben, are you alright?' Miss Mackenzie taught History as well as English. She gazed at me as I walked into her classroom. We had a double period of History after lunch. 'You look really pale.'

'I don't feel great,' I said honestly.

'Maybe you'd better go to sick bay,' she said, taking a step back from me as though I was contagious.

I nodded. Carrying my bag, I walked down the corridor and rounded a corner.

Of course I wasn't going to go to sick bay. Instead, I headed toward Mr Slender's classroom. Hopefully, I'd read the timetable right and it would be empty. If anyone was in there, my plan wouldn't work. I crept forward and peered through the window in the door.

A voice echoed down the corridor. 'Aha! Caught you!'

'AAARRRGGGHHH!' I jumped about a foot in the air.

'Sorry! I couldn't resist.' Mr Crumpet walked toward me. Corvus was perched on his

shoulder wearing his little hood. 'Shouldn't you be in class?'

'Yes … errr … no. I mean, I was just checking the timetable.' Glancing through the window, I caught a glimpse of Mr Slender sitting at his desk. And now I'd been busted!

'Is Mr Slender in there?' said Mr Crumpet.

'Um … I think so,' I said, already backing away.

'Hhmmph. Well, off you go then,' muttered Mr Crumpet. He turned and rapped on the door.

I walked fast; the last thing I wanted was for Mr Slender to see I'd been snooping around again. Luckily, I'd reached the end of the corridor by the time I heard him open the door. I slipped around the corner and stopped to listen.

'Sorry to disturb, old boy, but I wondered if you might have a minute to spare?' boomed Mr Crumpet's voice. 'They've put one of those newfangled whiteboards in my room. The thing's a mystery to me. Would you mind giving me a quick run-through?'

Mr Slender said something I couldn't quite catch. Then Mr Crumpet spoke again.

'Could we possibly do it in my room instead? That way we can get the thing set up too. Only if it's no trouble.'

The door closed. Then there was the sound of shoes tapping against the hard floor, heading in the opposite direction.

I lowered my backpack and peered around the wall. The two men were at the far end of the hallway. As I watched, they rounded the corner and were gone.

Taking a deep breath, I crept back toward Mr Slender's classroom. Suddenly, everything was back on track again. As I walked along, a strange feeling swept over me. It was a sort of tingling wave that went from my feet all the way to my head. I felt as though I was on the brink of discovering something amazing; something that would change my life forever.

If only I'd known how right I was.

12

The door to Mr Slender's classroom was unlocked. I opened it just wide enough to slip inside, and closed it silently behind me.

Through the walls, I could hear the faint sounds of other teachers talking and yelling. I knew that anyone walking past would be able to see me through the window so the sooner I was out of sight, the better.

I glanced around the room.

The cupboard was in the far corner, exactly where it was marked on the plan in Mr Knight's office. It was big for a cupboard; in fact, it was almost a small

room. Every classroom in the school had a cupboard like this one. Depending on the subject, inside them were art supplies or Bunsen burners or chisels or sewing machines.

I crept over to it. The door handle was stiff and, for a second, I thought it was locked, but suddenly it turned and the door creaked open. Light from the classroom spilled into the cupboard.

I ducked into it, shutting the door behind me. Instantly, everything went black. Trying not to freak out, I unzipped my bag and felt around inside. My hand closed over the torch. I switched it on and shone it around the small space. Now what?

I swept the beam of light across the shelves. They were made of dark timber and looked really ancient, like they had been there since the school was built. Worn textbooks, rulers and calculators were arranged in neat rows on them.

I peered closer, examining the shelves. The top and bottom ones were almost empty, and covered in a thick layer of dust. Except for one shelf.

This shelf was level with my chest. It was identical to all the others except that it was a bit less dusty. It held a row of books.

I shone my torch across them. One of the books was jutting out a bit further than the others. It looked exactly like the other books in the row, except that the top of the spine was worn away, as though someone had removed it from the shelf many times and, every single time, had grabbed it in

exactly the same spot. Written on the spine were the words: *Beyond Ordinary Logic*.

Tingles crept down my back.

I raised my hand, grasped the spine of the book, and pulled.

The book didn't come out; instead, it swung down. It was attached to the shelf at the base of its spine. Something deep within the walls clunked. There was the sound of cogs whirring.

Then, silence. I waited for a full minute, but nothing more happened.

Wondering what to do, I shone my torch into the corners of the shelves, looking for anything that seemed out of place. Then I peered at the edges of the shelves. That's when I saw it: one small section of the wood was completely dust-free. In fact, it looked as though it had been recently polished.

I rested my hand on it and pushed gently. The entire back wall of the cupboard swung open. A rush of stale air swept over me. I swayed backward and almost fell, partly from the gust of wind, but mostly from shock. Although I had thought I'd find another secret door, deep down I hadn't been certain. But here it was.

I shone the torch into the opening, which was a bit smaller than an ordinary doorway, and seemed to lead into a tunnel. The wooden floor of the cupboard continued for a short distance before dropping away. Beyond that, rough stone walls vanished down a dark tunnel. It was just like the entrance to the crypt in *Zombie Attack 1*. The only thing missing was a horde of undead!

Swallowing hard, I stepped through the doorway. Then stopped. What if Mr Slender came back, and checked in the cupboard? If the secret door was open, he would know someone had found it. I shivered at the thought.

Inside my bag I found a pencil. Working carefully, and with the torch clamped between my knees, I closed the bookcase door. But instead of letting it shut completely, I jammed the pencil between the door and the wall. Now, the door couldn't latch. Hopefully, if somebody was to look inside the cupboard, they wouldn't notice the door wasn't shut properly. And it wouldn't be too smart to lock myself in there anyway, I decided, as I zipped my bag shut and shone my torch in front of me.

I set off slowly. Where the wooden floor of the cupboard ended, the ground dropped

away to a set of stone stairs. The steps were steep and there were no handrails, only solid stone walls on either side. The tunnel looked really old, maybe even older than the school. I kept the beam of light on the floor so I wouldn't trip. Getting injured down here would be even worse than getting stuck in the cupboard. I might never get out!

The further down I went, the quieter it became. Soon there was no sound at all, except for a gurgling noise, like water running through a pipe.

When I reached the bottom of the steps, the tunnel became wider and little rooms branched off it on either side. I flashed the torch into them as I walked past. These rooms didn't seem to lead anywhere, and some of them had collapsed, leaving piles of stone and rubble on the ground. Why had someone built all this?

Up ahead, the tunnel forked into two. I stopped, wondering which way to go. Both tunnels looked exactly the same, which made me realise how easy it would be to get lost down here. I shuddered. Perhaps I should go back and tell Sophie about it? Now that I'd found a secret passageway, she would have to believe me! We could come down here together to explore the rest.

I turned to go back. But before I could take a step, I heard a distant noise — a faint clatter, like something had fallen onto the floor. My ears strained. I could hear myself breathing fast. Was someone down here? Or some*thing*?

Another sound rang out: footsteps on rock.

Someone was walking down the stairs toward me.

13

It was Slender. It had to be. I glanced around wildly. I had to make a run for it, but which way?

I'd read somewhere that when you were lost in a maze you should keep to one direction, either the left or the right, and you would eventually get out. I didn't really understand how that was supposed to work, but right then I didn't have any other ideas.

I chose the left-hand tunnel and started running.

It sounded like the footsteps were getting closer, although it was a bit hard to tell because I was breathing so hard. I came to another fork in the tunnel and again chose the left side. This tunnel was wider and, instead of little rooms, there were more tunnels branching off it. As I raced past their open, black mouths, cold air blew over me. I ditched my bag in an empty room and kept running.

But it didn't seem to matter how fast I went — the person, the *thing*, was gaining on me. A stitch formed in my side. I could hardly breathe. Then, out of nowhere, I was running on air. My torch went flying. I landed on my hands and knees.

But that wasn't the worst of it.

Before I could get up, there was a hideous screech and an enormous weight landed on my back, squashing me flat.

'AAAGGHHHH!' I heard someone scream and realised that it was me. Man! Did I really sound like that? 'AAAAGG-GGHHH!' I guess so.

'IT'S OOOOKKAAAAAYYYYYYY!' screamed another voice. 'It's MEEEEEE!'

It took a few seconds for me to realise that I hadn't been attacked by a Cannibal Corpse from *The Zombie Returns*. 'Sophie?'

By now she had climbed off me and was dusting herself down. 'Thanks for breaking my fall. Are you OK?'

'I think so.' I was still pretty shaken by the whole thing, but I didn't seem to have any injuries other than the gravel rash on my palms and knees, which I had scraped pretty badly on the rocky ground. I clambered to my feet, found the torch, and shone it on the ground behind to see what had tripped us. It was a steep step.

I turned to Sophie. 'What are you doing down here? How did you find me?'

'When I realised you'd left History early, I guessed you had gone to Mr Slender's room to check out the cupboard. I noticed your pencil wedged between the wall and the door, so I pushed it open and followed the sound of your footsteps.'

'So you believe me now?'

'Sure.' Sophie found the Fuzzil, which had fallen off her shoulder, and as she stuck it back onto her collar she muttered, 'Sorry.'

'That's OK,' I said. Secretly, I was relieved to see her. 'Anyway, I dunno if we should go any further. We don't want to get lost.'

'Let's go back and check out the other tunnel,' said Sophie, turning back the way we'd come. 'The big one with the light.'

'What one with the light?' I asked. How did I miss that?

'It's just back here.'

For the first time, I noticed she held a small torch. 'Did you bring that?' I asked as I trotted along behind.

'Nah. Found it in Slender's cupboard,' she explained. 'I guess he uses it when he comes down here.'

As we walked, I realised that the ground was sloping slightly upward, which I hadn't noticed while I'd been running. We were also a lot further into the tunnels than I'd thought.

After a few minutes Sophie stopped before the mouth of a tunnel that branched off to the right. I peered into the opening; it was bigger than any of the other tunnels I'd seen. A strange smell drifted from it and there was a sound too, although one I didn't recognise. It was a high-pitched screeching sound, like fingernails running down a blackboard.

'C'mon.' Sophie began walking down the tunnel.

Nervously, I followed. Around the first bend, the tunnel widened even further. On either side, old wooden doors were placed at regular intervals, some shut, some slightly ajar. I opened one. Inside was a small room. It was empty except for a pile of bricks in one corner where part of the wall had collapsed.

'Come on!' hissed Sophie impatiently.

I closed the door and we kept walking until we rounded another corner.

A pair of big metal doors stood in front of us. They were tightly closed, but on one door, about halfway up, was an enormous old latch with a key jutting out of it.

Above the doors was a sign.

'What does *Rattus* mean?' asked Sophie.

'I'm not sure,' I said, feeling pretty certain I didn't want to find out. Then, before I could stop her, Sophie reached out and turned the key.

14

She pushed the doors open.

The sound and smell hit me at the same time. It was like we had walked into a sewer filled with howling ghosts. I tried not to be sick, although I couldn't stop the hairs on the back of my neck from standing upright.

'It's OK,' said Sophie. Her face was stark white. 'They're in cages.'

Even though every instinct in my body told me to run away, I edged forward.

Through the doorway was a big room. I shone my torch around; the walls were made of stone, just like the tunnels, and

they were lined with cages stacked two or three high. Inside these were rats.

Now I haven't seen that many rats in my time, but these were nothing like the friendly white rats that are sold in pet stores. These guys were huge and grey and covered with patchy fur. Their eyes were bright red and some of them had bits missing; a leg here, an ear there. As the beams from our torches swept over them, they snarled and turned away from the light.

We crept further into the room. I noticed that every cage had a plastic water dispenser attached to it. Most of the dispensers were full.

'Who put these animals here?' I asked.

'And how did they do it?' said Sophie. 'I wouldn't be game to try to catch rats like these.'

The rats sniffed the air as we walked past, and began flinging themselves at the bars of their cages. Some of them ripped at the metal with their teeth or tried to squeeze through the gaps.

'They can smell us,' I said, watching a rat that seemed desperate to get at us. We'd get eaten alive if they managed to get out of their cages!

'I think they have rage issues,' agreed Sophie. 'Hey, look at this.' She pointed the beam of her torch above the cages.

shuffle shuffle

Scrawled in chalk on the stone wall opposite us was the word 'half'. On the wall nearest us was the word 'full'. 'The "full" ones look way scarier than the "half" ones.'

I gazed at the rats. She was right. The 'half' rats looked *almost* normal. I mean,

they were still freaky and their eyes were still red, but they weren't quite as big and ragged. And they didn't look as vicious.

I shone my torch across to the far end of the room.

'Look!'

In the middle of the back wall was another set of doors, like the ones we'd just walked through. Then I noticed the sign above them. I walked over to the doors and peered upward. I could just make out the words:

Canis Iupus familiaris

'What does that mean?' asked Sophie, her voice shaking.

I didn't answer. Surely it couldn't be worse than the rats, could it?

I turned the key this time. My hands were shaking so much I could hardly move my fingers. I slowly opened the doors.

The hairs on the back of my neck leapt straight up; inside the room, it sounded like a thousand zombies were screaming for brains! The smell was just as bad as the rat room, but this time the cages were bigger — and so were the animals in them.

'Dogs,' breathed Sophie.

They were snarling and growling and pacing around their cages. Like the rats, their eyes glowed bright red. We edged inside.

'They're bulldogs,' she said. 'My next-door neighbour used to have one.'

'Do they like bulls?' I asked.

Sophie smiled nervously. 'No. They were used to hunt them. The dogs would track them by following their scent.'

I shuddered.

There were at least twenty dogs in cages. Instead of being stacked, the cages stood alongside each other on the floor. Their doors were attached to black chains that stretched up and disappeared toward the ceiling. That must be how the dogs are put into the cages, I thought. *Or let out of them.*

Just the thought of the dogs being let out made me want to pee myself.

'They're not that bad,' said Sophie, looking into a big cage that contained three dogs. 'I think they're kind of cute.'

'Yeah. If you like animals that want to tear you apart for fun!'

She ignored me. 'Look! That one wants to play with his ball.'

I stared. 'That's not a ball.'

'Ewwww!' said Sophie, backing away.

We wandered around the room, staring at the animals. Why would someone want to keep all these dogs? And what was *wrong* with them?

'How do you think they got like this?' I said.

'I don't know …' Sophie began, as she went over to the far corner of the room. Then she stopped. 'Hang on, I think I've just found the answer.'

I walked over to where she stood in front of an old table. On it was a bottle.

She lifted it up. Brownish liquid swirled around inside it.

'There's a tag,' she said, peering at a bit of paper tied to the neck of the bottle. She read aloud: '"Formula 1037 — USE WITH CAUTION! EFFECT IS IMMEDIATE AND PERMANENT!"'

'Is it some sort of medicine?' I asked.

'I don't think so,' said Sophie. She put the bottle back down carefully. 'I think they've all been given this.

I think it's what turned them into …
something else.'

'What *are* they?' I said, staring at the
creatures that had once been dogs.

'I'm not sure exactly,' said Sophie in a
shaking voice. 'But I think we should get
out of here before whoever did this to them
comes back.'

15

I didn't need any convincing. I turned toward the big metal doors where we'd entered the chamber. Then stopped.

'I can't remember closing the doors,' I said. Even to my own ears, my voice sounded small and scared.

'Me neither,' said Sophie. She grabbed one of the wooden door handles. 'It's locked!'

'Get out of the way,' I said. I was really starting to freak out. I closed my fingers tightly around the door handle and pulled as hard as I could. Nothing happened. I put one foot up on the other door for extra leverage. I tried pushing instead of pulling. Still the door didn't budge. 'Holy cow!' I said finally. 'It's locked.'

'That's what I said.' Sophie sounded annoyed, but I knew she was freaking out too. 'We're locked in a secret chamber deep underground. Nobody knows where we are. Nobody will ever find us.'

'It's not that bad,' I said, trying to sound brave. 'Whoever has been looking after the dogs will have to come back to feed them. They'll find us then.'

Sophie looked at me with her mouth

hanging open. 'Great! We'll be found by a madman who turns animals into monsters! That's exactly the sort of person I'd like to avoid!'

'Hey, I'm just trying to make you feel better!' Girls! No matter what you did for them, they were never grateful! 'Anyway, there must be another way out of here.'

It didn't take us long to find it. Another pair of metal doors, even bigger and stronger-looking than the ones we'd just walked through, stood at the other end of the room. There were at least a dozen big bolts around the latch, which again had an old key sticking out of it.

'What does it say?' I asked, pointing my torch above the doors.

We squinted upward through the darkness. Visible faintly in the dim light was another sign.

Homo Sapiens

'That sounds familiar,' Sophie said uncertainly. 'I'm not sure if we should go in there.'

'We don't have much choice,' I told her.

It took us ages to draw back all the bolts and, the whole time, my heart was thumping. Finally, it was time to turn the enormous key.

I looked at Sophie. She gave a little nod. Whatever was inside the room, we would meet it together.

Side by side, we turned the key and pushed the doors open.

Before us lay a huge chamber. Flaming torches were dotted around the walls and a stone platform stood at the far end. Along the walls were more cages, bigger than the

ones used for the dogs. Luckily, they were empty.

'What is this place?' whispered Sophie.

I walked closer to the cages. There were a dozen altogether, each standing taller than a man. A chain was attached to the bars at the back of each cage. These chains were connected to sets of shackles.

At first, I thought all the cages were identical, but then I noticed one that was different. This one stood a little apart from the others. Above its door was a sign.

As I read the words, my knees went weak.

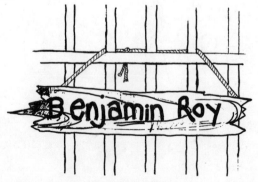

The sign above the cage had my name on it. That could only mean one thing.

'It's meant for me.' My voice sounded like it was coming from some other place.

Sophie made a choking sound. 'Why would anyone want to put you in a cage?'

Suddenly, there was flash of movement in front of us. A figure strode onto the stone platform.

'Welcome! I've been expecting you.'

I could feel my face turning white with shock.

'You!' gasped Sophie.

16

It was Mr Crumpet. As usual, Corvus sat on his shoulder, but for the first time the bird wasn't wearing his usual hood.

'Welcome to my little experiment! Don't look so surprised — surely you must have figured it out by now.'

'What …? Why …?' I stuttered.

'Dear oh dear! We are slow off the mark.' Crumpet strutted up and down like a performer on a stage. 'Don't tell me you

still haven't got a clue what's going on. Good grief! And to think that, at one point, I thought you might be on to me.'

'You? How can it be you?' Sophie said. She looked as stunned as I felt.

'Who else could it be?' snapped Mr Crumpet, glaring at her. 'Nobody else around here could pull it off. Nobody! Do you know how difficult it was? How many rats I went through before I stumbled across the key ingredient that made everything work together? But the chemistry is perfect now! It reads like a masterpiece. And you,' he said as he pointed at me, 'you are the lucky one.'

'Me …?' I stammered.

'Oh, I know you don't deserve it — I mean you're nothing special, are you? You're small for your age and not very smart, as it turns out. You're really not much good at

anything at all. But that's exactly why you've been chosen! I wanted someone who could disappear easily. Someone who wouldn't be missed.' He waved his hand dismissively. 'Sure, your parents will be a bit upset at first. But after a year or two, you'll fade from everyone's minds. People will think you were just a runaway.'

'You chose me? For what?' My knees felt like they were going to collapse under me.

'To join the ranks of the immortal,' said Mr Crumpet, staring at me with his pale blue eyes. 'To become *more than human*!'

'To become a zombie, that's what you mean!' shouted Sophie. 'If you want to

experiment, do it on yourself and leave him alone!'

Mr Crumpet turned his icy stare on her. 'Oh, but it's not just him, young lady. You have an important part to play too. A very important part. In fact, some might say it will be you making … What do they call it? Oh yes, *the ultimate sacrifice*! You will make the ultimate sacrifice for the good of science.'

Sophie opened her mouth, but no sound came out.

'Don't look so upset!' cried Mr Crumpet. 'This is a great day for science and it's a great day for you. Oh, how I worried that it wouldn't happen at all!'

'You won't get away with this,' I said, hoping I sounded braver than I felt. Could this really be happening? Maybe I'd played one zombie game too many and was stuck in some weird zombie dream!

'I won't?' Crumpet raised his eyebrows at me. 'Does anyone know you are here?'

'Yes!' I lied, my heart sinking. Why hadn't I told anyone else about the secret door?

'I doubt that,' said Mr Crumpet with another of his thin, sharp smiles. 'I doubt that very much.'

'It's true! Mr Slender knows we're down here.' I was pretty sure Mr Slender had no idea where we were, but I was prepared to try anything.

'Slender?' snapped Mr Crumpet. 'Yes, he's been a bit of a complication. He's been poking around ever since I set up

that little trap under the stairs. You don't know how disappointed I was that it didn't work!'

'What trap?' I said.

'After sending you to the toilets to wash your knee, I slipped into the janitor's storeroom, leaving the door open a crack. I knew you'd notice it and curiosity would get the better of you. I was right, of course. In you wandered and, all the while, I was watching you through a crack between the boards beyond the second secret door. I opened it briefly, hoping you would be silly enough to venture down to the tunnels and into my clutches. But then Slender appeared and I had to abort the plan.'

'But how did you know we would come down here today?' I asked, trying to keep him talking.

'When I caught you outside Mr Slender's room after lunch, I guessed you'd figured out there was another secret door, and you were trying to make your move during Slender's free period. That's why I made up the story about the whiteboard — to draw him away from his room so you could get into the tunnel. By the time he'd finished poking around trying to get the thing set up, you were well and truly in my trap.'

'But …' I groped around. I had to buy more time so I could figure out a plan. 'If it's so great to be a zombie, why don't you become one yourself?'

'Some day, that's exactly what I'll do. But first, the Master wants me to create an army for him. A zombie army!'

'The Master?'

'The one I serve. Shhhhh!' Suddenly, Crumpet looked frightened. He glanced

around wildly. 'The Master will hear you. The Master hears everything! It's time we finished this. It's time you became a zombie!'

Mr Crumpet lifted the raven off his shoulder. 'Corvus! Attack!'

17

The bird gave a squawk and spread his giant wings. With a couple of huge beats, he had launched himself into the air and was flying straight toward me.

For the first time, I saw his eyes. They were bright red. I think he was screeching, but I couldn't hear him. I couldn't hear anything!

He swooped at me. I ducked. His wings brushed against my hair, and he was soaring back up and around the roof of the chamber.

'ATTACK! ATTACK!' screamed Mr Crumpet.

'Let's get out of here!' I shouted.

Sophie didn't need to be told twice. We bolted toward the door.

But Corvus was already flying back toward us. I ducked again, but this time the raven was ready for it. He swooped lower and landed on my shoulder. His talons sunk into my skin.

'AAAAGGGHHHH!' I screamed and crashed to the ground. I tried to tear him off me, but the bird was really strong, like

he had some sort of superpower. It was then I realised: Corvus was a zombie too!

'Get off him!' Sophie was screaming. She tried to push the bird away, but even with both of us trying, we couldn't budge him.

Suddenly, Corvus started pecking at my neck. Pain shot through my body. Blood ran down my shoulder.

'CORVUS!' Mr Crumpet's voice echoed through the chamber. 'ENOUGH!'

The bird tightened his grip on my shoulder, then launched himself upward.

'Aaaggghhh …' I rolled over and tried to sit up.

'Are you OK?' Sophie's worried face swam before me.

'He's better than OK,' said Mr Crumpet. His voice seemed to come from far away. 'He's more than human now. He's the first of our great army.'

Something weird was happening to me. It was like I had poked my fingers into a power socket and waves of electricity were rippling through me. I couldn't move.

'Don't be alarmed!' said Mr Crumpet, walking closer. Corvus was on his shoulder again. 'The virus has been transferred to you from the bird's saliva. It's travelling through your bloodstream as we speak. Soon, your body will be ten times stronger than before. You will be able to run faster than any other human being. And, best of all, you will feel nothing for your own kind. No empathy, no guilt. Only hunger!'

Agonising pain rippled up and down my body. I couldn't get enough air.

'You will be consumed by your own hunger for human flesh! Nothing else will satisfy you!'

'You're crazy!' screamed Sophie, but I could see her looking at me with fear in her eyes.

I tried to speak. I tried to tell Sophie to run. But all that came out was: 'Nnnggghhh!' Something was happening to me. I was changing. Adrenaline was surging through my body. I felt like my muscles were about to burst through my skin.

'The virus only does half the job,' said Mr Crumpet matter-of-factly. 'You may

not have noticed, but I've marked the cages. Some of the beasts have been infected, but haven't made their first kill. They are only half-zombies. They still have the powers of a zombie — strength, speed, infrared vision — but they haven't got the mindless killing instinct of a full zombie. That only happens when a zombie breaks that final taboo and kills one of its own kind. Only then do they become full zombies.' He swung his pale gaze onto Sophie. 'That's why you are so important, my dear. That's why you'll be making the ultimate sacrifice.'

Sophie screamed. She turned to run, but Corvus was flying through the air toward her. Without warning, he landed on her back. Sophie toppled forward. I heard something hit the ground with a sickening thud.

And then she lay still.

The room spun around me and everything went black.

18

When I woke, the weird feeling was gone. I sat up and looked around. Where was I? *Who* was I? Stone walls surrounded me. A man with a bird on his shoulder stood at a distance. For some reason I felt like I should know who he was. But I couldn't remember anything.

Power rippled through my body. I felt incredibly strong.

The man stared at me.

'Eat!' he hissed, pointing at something on the ground nearby.

I suddenly realised how hungry I was. I was starving! I had to eat right now!

And the only thing I wanted was meat.

I crawled toward the thing on the floor. I could smell it was meat. I could smell everything. The scent of fear hung thickly in the air. A waft of excitement drifted in a stream from the strange man with the bird. I could smell hunger too; the hunger of dogs and the hunger of rats.

But mostly, I could smell my own hunger. It was so strong! I could almost taste the meat in my mouth. I could feel the juices running down my chin. I had to have it now!

'Eat!' urged the man again.

I drew closer. The meat was so warm and fresh! I could smell it was still alive, but I didn't care. Eating it would take care of that problem!

I leant forward to take a bite, but suddenly it moved. I jumped back. The

meat groaned and rolled over. I could see its face now. Its skin was pale and blood was seeping out from under it. Suddenly, I wasn't hungry anymore.

'EAT! EAT!' screamed the man.

I gazed at the meat. 'Sophie,' I said. Where had that word come from? I wiped the blood off its face.

I didn't want to eat this meat. In fact, this wasn't meat at all. This was my friend!

'EAT HER! YOU MUST CONSUME HER FLESH!' The man had gone red in the face and was dancing from one foot to the other.

'No!' I said. 'She's my friend!'

'No?' asked the man. 'You don't say no to me! You are a minion in the Master's army now. A slave! Nothing more! Now eat!'

'No,' I said again. I could smell the man's anger now.

'She cannot leave the chamber alive,' said the man. 'So if you don't kill her, something else will.'

He strode over to a metal bar attached to the back wall, grasped it with both hands and pulled down. There was the sound of metal grinding and then another sound: the scratching of claws against stone.

And then a pack of zombie bulldogs burst through the door.

Their smell was like a river of blood and hunger and fury. But, somehow, I knew

they wouldn't hurt me. They could sense I was one of them now. They were only interested in Sophie.

'No!' I rushed forward and knelt over her. How could I stop them? There were too many for me to kill!

'Get back! Let them have her!' said the man.

I stared at him. Suddenly, it all came rushing back. Mr Crumpet! He had trapped us down here, deep underground. He had made his bird attack me and infect me with the zombie virus. And, after this was over, he would go back upstairs and pretend that nothing was wrong, that he had no idea where we were. And meanwhile, Sophie would be dead and I would be locked down here in a cage. Forever.

I looked back down at Sophie. Her Fuzzil had come unstuck from her shoulder

and was sitting in a little puddle of blood beside her head.

I grabbed the blood-soaked Fuzzil.

I stood up and bowled it along the ground. It rolled across the chamber, leaving behind a faint trail of blood. Without the extra strength in my arms, it probably wouldn't have made it. But it did. Just. It hit the back of Mr Crumpet's shoe, then bounced up and stuck to the leg of his trousers — exactly where I'd been aiming.

I turned back to the dogs. They had almost reached us. I could see their bared teeth and their mad red eyes. Quickly, I slid my arms under Sophie. As I lifted her above my head, the dogs fell upon us.

The bulldogs swarmed around me,

snarling at me, but not attacking. In fact, some of them cowered away from me, as though they sensed I was more powerful than they were.

They smelt the ground where Sophie had been lying only a second ago. Instantly, they found the small puddle of blood. There was a flash of teeth and a yelp and it was gone. Then they sniffed around until one of them picked up the faint trail of blood.

After that, it all happened very fast.

As one, the pack of hounds followed the trail. By the time Mr Crumpet realised, it was too late. The dogs leapt on him and he vanished beneath the pile of wriggling, growling fur.

nom! nom! nom!

19

While the dogs were distracted, I carried Sophie through the large metal doors, stopping for a moment to put her down and shut them behind us. I drew all the bolts, just to be sure. The next set of doors — the ones we couldn't budge before — opened easily this time. At first I couldn't understand why, and then I remembered: I was super strong now.

It was darker in this room so I moved carefully. Weirdly, the rats were silent as they watched me carrying Sophie past their cages. At first I thought it was because I was one of them now, and somehow they

could sense it. But then I realised that we weren't alone. Something had followed us out, slipping along behind us, unseen and silent, as we made our escape. Carefully, I put Sophie down again. Then I turned to face it.

It was Corvus. I waved my arm at him.

'Go away! Get lost, you creepy thing!' I hadn't forgot how he'd torn at the skin

on my neck. I felt around under my t-shirt, but I couldn't find where the bird had pecked me. The wound was gone. Did being a zombie mean I had some sort of healing ability? That would be handy! There was still a little blood on my neck so I wiped it with the inside of my shirt.

Corvus soared around the roof, squawking down at me. I ignored him and picked up Sophie again, then pushed through the last pair of doors into the tunnel. The bird slipped through before I could stop him. He flew ahead and vanished into the darkness.

In the tunnel I groped my way along slowly. I didn't want to trip and drop Sophie.

I had walked only a few steps when it happened: a bright-blue light suddenly flashed around me. It flickered a few times,

and then everything was glowing! The brick walls on either side of the tunnel were blue. The stone roof was purple. Sophie glowed with a bright-yellow light that seemed to come from somewhere inside her. It was amazing! But where was the light coming from?

I thought about what Mr Crumpet had said just after Corvus had bitten me. I was a half-zombie now, which meant I had speed, strength and *infrared vision*!

For a while my eyes kept jumping back and forth between ordinary and infrared vision. I'd need to practise before I'd be able to control it. But finally the infrared vision stayed on and I began to jog, and then to sprint. Sophie felt as light as a feather as I zoomed through the tunnels. It only took a couple of minutes before I reached the stone staircase that led to

Slender's cupboard. I raced up, two at a time. At the top, I could see an outline of daylight around the secret door. I put Sophie down and felt around the edges for a latch or handle, but couldn't find anything.

I was just about to try to break it down, when I realised I could smell something. Human skin. I sniffed around and traced the smell to a small latch on the wall beside the door. That must be how Mr Crumpet opened it from this side, I realised. I poked my fingers into the latch and pressed. Something clunked inside the wall and the door creaked open. Lifting Sophie carefully, I stepped into the cupboard.

The light was intense! I had to close my eyes. There was a weird feeling behind my lids, like something was sliding across my eyeballs. Then, when I opened my eyes

again, my normal vision was back. But now everything was so dark I could hardly see at all.

The cupboard door stood wide open, and moonlight flooded in through the windows of the classroom. I guessed that with infrared vision, even the tiniest bit of light was super bright. I was going to have to get better at controlling my new abilities.

I carried Sophie through the cupboard and put her down on the floor of Mr Slender's room. As I lowered her, she stirred.

'What happened?'

'It's OK,' I said. 'We got away.'

She rubbed her head. 'Ouch! Away from what? Where are we?'

'You banged your head,' I told her. 'Don't worry, I carried you out of the tunnel. We're safe now.'

'The tunnel?' Sophie glared at me. 'You're not still going on about that, are you? We've already searched for the tunnel, remember? It wasn't there!'

Oh man! Where was the gratitude?

But then a thought crept into my mind: maybe it was better if she couldn't remember. Maybe if people knew I was a zombie — even just a half-zombie — it would totally freak them out!

'Yeah,' I said slowly. 'You're right. You fell over in the … cupboard while we were searching for another secret door.'

'I knew it!' She peered at me. 'Your eyes look really red, like you've been crying. Were you upset that I got hurt?'

As if! I blinked and looked away. I hadn't

even thought about my eyes! Hopefully they weren't glowing as red as the zombie animals'. How was I going to explain that?

'It's OK,' said Sophie, smiling a bit. 'You can admit it! You were totally upset that I got hurt, weren't you?'

I had to force myself to say it. 'Yes,' I muttered.

Sophie looked pleased. Then she winced. 'Ouch! I must've fallen hard! ' She rubbed her head. 'How did you manage to pick me up?'

'Well …' I thought fast. 'I didn't exactly pick you up, I just kind of dragged you out here.'

'That's why I'm all dirty!' Sophie dusted her knees.

'Yeah,' I said. Then, because I was pretty keen to change the subject, I added, 'Let's get out of here.'

I helped her to her feet, being careful not to reveal my new strength. With her arm draped over my shoulder, we reached the door. Just as I was about to turn the knob, it swung open. A figure loomed over us.

'Aha! I've found you!'

20

'Everyone's been searching for you,' said Mr Slender, as he peered down at us. 'I hope you haven't been in any trouble?'

'Umm …' I said, wishing I had time to think up a reason for our disappearance and wondering when people would notice Mr Crumpet was missing.

'I fell,' said Sophie. 'Look.' She reached over and flicked the light switch. Mr Slender gasped.

Sophie's hair dangled in clumps around her face and dried blood was smeared down her cheek. Suddenly, her knees seemed to give way. She moaned weakly.

'I think I need some help here,' I lied, pretending to struggle under her weight.

Mr Slender grabbed Sophie by her other arm, and we steered her into the corridor. 'Everyone's been worried about you both. What happened?'

'We were looking for something,' I said, thinking fast. 'But we couldn't find it so we were checking the cupboard in case it had been put away. Sophie climbed up the shelves, and that's when she fell.'

'But …' said Mr Slender.

'Is that Mum and Dad?' I interrupted. I didn't want to answer any more awkward questions!

'Yes. Everyone's here,' said Mr Slender. His lips were in a thin line. I could see he didn't believe my excuse.

'Benjamin!' Mum rushed up to us and flung her arms around me. I tried to wriggle free. I couldn't breathe.

'Mum! Need air!' I gasped.

She crushed me tighter against her bosom. 'My little Benny! I was so worried about you!'

I took a quick gulp of oxygen before I was buried in the folds of her dress again.

'Where have you been? What happened?' she asked.

'Nuublthindg. We'bre obay. Honeslhhtlky, id's ndo big deal.'

'What? I can't understand a word you're saying!' Mum finally let me go.

'We're fine, Mum!' I said.

'Well! If that's the case, you are in so much trouble, young man!'

What? How did that work? 'Actually, I think I've hurt my ankle,' I said quickly. I limped a bit.

Mum looked worried again. 'Which one?'

'Don't fall for it, Mum.' Michael appeared behind her. 'It's Sophie who looks like she's had a run-in with Tank!'

'What happened to her?' asked Dad.

'SOPHIE!' screamed another voice as Sophie's parents came running down the hall.

'I'm OK,' said Sophie. Then she added, 'I fell, but Ben looked after me.'

Mrs Knight gazed at me with teary eyes. 'Thanks, Ben! You're a good friend.'

'It was nothing,' I said. I almost felt guilty; if it hadn't been for me, Sophie wouldn't have got hurt at all.

'Sophie fell off the shelves inside my classroom cupboard,' said Mr Slender. He shot a meaningful look at Mr Knight.

Mr Knight glared at me. 'What did I tell you about poking around old cupboards?'

'Ummmm,' I said.

'Leave the poor wee lad alone!' Before I could stop her, Mrs Knight squashed me against *her* bosom. 'He's been through enough!'

I tried to fight my way free, but that only made things worse.

'The main thing is that everyone is alive and well,' said Dad, as I gasped for air. 'Let's go home.'

As we walked home, we were told the whole story. After it had got dark, Mum and Dad had rung Sophie's parents, and when they realised we weren't there all four of them had walked around, checking the back yards and the parks and all the other places we usually hang out. It was only when they were getting desperate that they finally rang the school and made their way there.

'You know there are old tunnels under your school,' said Mr Knight, as we walked back through the dark streets toward their house. 'I'm researching them for my next book.'

'Oh really?' I said, trying to sound

casual. So *that's* why he had those maps in his bus.

'They were constructed during the Spanish flu epidemic, around 1918. Seabrook was first built as a hospital, to quarantine sick people. But they needed a cold place to store the dead bodies so they dug out a morgue underneath. That's what the tunnels were used for.'

Sophie shivered. 'Ewww!'

'When the Spanish flu epidemic was over, they didn't really need the hospital anymore so they turned it into a school. A team of people was sent down to explore the tunnels, but they never returned. People started saying there were monsters or zombies living in the tunnels and in the end they were blocked off.'

'Creepy!' I said. So that was why he had the pictures of zombies. But it still

didn't explain why he was so jumpy about people going in his bus. Or why he nearly strangled me in the yard!

Maybe he realised what I was thinking 'cause he added, 'I'm trying to keep what I'm writing a secret so the kids at school don't find out about the tunnels and decide to take a look themselves. Poking around these old buildings isn't safe.'

'So how did Sophie bang her head?' asked Mrs Knight.

I tried to keep my voice offhand. 'I left her Fuzzil in Mr Slender's room during detention. He must have put it in the cupboard. We went in there to see if we could find it and Sophie tried to climb up the shelves, but then she slipped.'

'I thought those little toys were supposed to be lucky!' said Mrs Knight.

'Maybe they bring *bad* luck,' said Mum.

Everybody laughed, but I didn't. The Fuzzil *had* been lucky! Without it, I don't know what I would have done to save Sophie from the zombie dogs.

We stopped outside Sophie's house.

'Thanks again, Ben,' said Mrs Knight. She gave me another quick hug.

Mr Knight ruffled my hair.

'Wanna come over tomorrow?' asked Sophie. 'I've got *Zombie Attack 3*, remember?'

I thought for a second. 'Maybe we can just ride our bikes instead.'

Sophie looked at me like I'd gone crazy.

After we said goodbye, we headed home. Mum and Dad walked ahead, holding hands.

Suddenly, everything flashed blue. My eyes switched back and forth a couple of times before settling on infrared vision. It

was so weird! I could see Mum's and Dad's hearts glowing white inside their bodies. Yellow and pink light radiated out from inside their bodies. It looked awesome!

Suddenly, I saw a purplish light circling high above us. I gazed up at it. Corvus! The bird had followed me here!

Corvus flew silently overhead. I guessed he wanted to hang out with me, now that I was a zombie too. Hopefully, Mum would be OK with me having such a weird pet.

Michael sidled up to me. 'I thought you'd disappeared for good.'

'No such luck,' I told him. 'I plan to hang around forever. You'll never get rid of me.'

'Wanna bet? Race you home! On your marks … get set …' Suddenly, he tore off down the street.

'Cheat!' I shouted. For a second I felt annoyed. Then I smiled; Michael was about to get a surprise.

By the time he jogged up to our house, I was sitting on the front step.

'When did you get so fast?' he puffed.

'I've been letting you win for years,' I lied.

He pulled a face and punched me in the arm. 'Ouch!' He shook his hand. 'Man! You're as hard as a rock!'

I tried not to smile. Life was going to be a lot more interesting as a zombie!

ZOMBIEFIED! INFECTED

Benjamin Roy is now a zombie … well, a half-zombie to be precise.

The trouble is he can't tell anyone about his new infrared vision and super-speed. Not even his best friend, Sophie. 'Cause he's pretty sure the government or the police or, even worse, his *parents* will lock him up if they find out.

But then someone starts watching him. And following him.

Somebody knows his secret. And unless Ben can figure out who it is, he'll have to start running. Or lurching really fast.

The adventure continues in January 2016 …